THE CONCEITED TURKEY
and other stories

by Sergio Bitossi

Translated and adapted by
Ann Macleod

Illustrated by S. Weigel

HAMLYN
London · New York · Sydney · Toronto

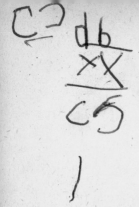

Published 1970 by
THE HAMLYN PUBLISHING GROUP LIMITED
London · New York · Sydney · Toronto
Hamlyn House, Feltham, Middlesex, England
for Golden Pleasure Books Limited
© Copyright Éditions des Deux Coqs d'Or, Paris, 1967, and
Mondadori-O.G.A.M. (Verona)
© Copyright English text Golden Pleasure Books Limited 1970
SBN 601 07359 2
Printed in Italy

Contents

The Lazy Snake 9
Cecil Takes a Photograph 12
The Swallow and the Fisherman 17
The Lighthouse in the Moon 24
Flatbill 28
The Little Stray Cat 33
The Proud Little Ant 35
The Story of a Red Balloon 40
The Bear and the Queen Bee 44
The Wicked Wolf 51
Jackie and the Thieving Magpie 57
The King's Banquet 63
The Conceited Turkey 68
Ping, Pong and Pang 73

The Frog's Lullaby 79
Tinker the Dog and Zoe the Flea 83
Bimgobo's Trick 89
St Nicholas and the Lemons 95
The Clown's Birthday Cake 99
Longtail, Tabbycat and the
 Gruyere Cheese 104
The Spider's Ointment 110
The Black Chick and the Fox 114
Aunt Marianne and the Prince 123
Golden Horns the Fawn 129
The Coachman's Wig 136
The Ghost in the Attic 142
The Adventures of Flop 157
Baptiste's Donkey 165
The Prince Who Yawned 171
The Liar's Soup 177
The Owl and the Chaffinch 180
The Baby Camel 184

The Lazy Snake

Once upon a time there was a snake-charmer who, morning and evening, made his cobra dance to the tune of his flute to delight the crowds of people thronging the market place.

But one day, the cobra felt very lazy and decided not to dance any more.

'Oh, master,' she said, 'I find I am growing as deaf as a post and I can no

9

longer hear the sound of your flute, so I shall not be able to dance any more.'

Having said this, she curled up in her basket feeling very pleased at her cleverness, and went to sleep.

She did not wake until lunchtime the next day and by then she felt very hungry and thirsty indeed.

'Hey, master!' she said. 'Why did you not give me my breakfast? I can hear the clock striking twelve. It is almost lunchtime.'

The snake-charmer smiled to himself at the way in which the cobra had betrayed herself.

'Ah, my poor snake, are you talking to me?' he asked. 'I am afraid you are wasting your breath for, curiously enough, I too am as deaf as a post!'

Cecil Takes a Photograph

For his birthday Cecil the chick was given a magnificent camera. All the birds in the farmyard clustered around him, begging him to take their photographs. There was Isabella the hen, William the drake, Marianne the goose, and many others. They pushed and shoved each other, squawking loudly:

'Take my photograph first!'

'No, it's my turn, take mine!'

'I photograph so well.'

'Oh, Cecil, please take a beautiful photo of me showing my beak in profile.'

Cecil, happy and smiling, promised that everyone should have a photo taken on his new camera. But just as Veronica the hen posed for the first picture, a beautiful ear of corn tucked under her wing Joseph the cock strutted up. He crowed so loudly that all the other birds had to clap their wings over their ears.

'Aha! I seem to be just in time to have my picture taken,' he said to Cecil, snatching an ear of corn from a terrified pullet. He fluttered up into the cherry tree and perched proudly on a slender branch.

14

Cecil and the other birds were much too frightened of the cock to think of arguing with him.

With trembling wings Cecil looked through his view-finder at Joseph, perched on the bough. Joseph looked very fine with his red comb and his feathers glistening in the sun.

'How do I look?' asked Joseph. 'Can you see me in your camera, little Cecil?'

'Could you move a little further along the branch, sir? Your tail is not in the picture,' said Cecil.

Joseph moved further along.

'Is that better?' he asked.

'Oh dear, now your beak will be left out. Please, could you move a bit further along?'

15

But Joseph had reached the very end of the branch and he was so heavy that the branch snapped under his weight. Bumpety-bump! Down to the ground fell Joseph, landing in a mass of feathers, amid the laughter of all the other birds. He hurried away, much ashamed, and never asked to be photographed again.

The Swallow and the Fisherman

Once a swallow was sunning herself on a telegraph wire when she heard a message being sent over the wire. This is what it said:

TO THE HARBOURMASTER. URGENT. FIND FISHERMAN SEBASTIAN. HIS SON IS GRAVELY ILL. VERY URGENT.

'How terrible!' thought the swallow. 'Suppose Sebastian should not hear the message? His little son wants him and he may never know. I will try and find him myself.'

Then the swallow spread her wings and flew over the great ocean, looking for fishing boats. Whenever she saw one she would fly down and perch on the poop and listen to the sailors or the fishermen as they talked to one another, hoping to hear the name Sebastian.

She heard all kinds of names, some of which she knew and others which were strange to her, but never once did she find a fisherman called Sebastian.

After a few days of searching the swallow was hungry and exhausted, but she would not give up. At last, she spied a very small boat, painted green and black and called *Madelaine*. There was only one man in it—a tall, sunburnt man who wore a red hat and smoked a pipe as he sat with the tiller under his arm. The swallow flew down and perched on the prow.

'Hello, little swallow,' said the man. 'You must be very far from home. What are you doing so far from land? Stay here with old Sebastian for a while, for I can see how tired you are. You need not be frightened of me.'

When she heard the name Sebastian, the swallow gave a loud chirrup. She flew on to the fisherman's shoulder and gently pecked his ear. Then she flew over to the boat's radio and perched there, looking hopefully at Sebastian.

'You funny little bird!' exclaimed the fisherman, laughing. 'Do you want to listen to the radio? Is it music you like? All right then. I'll switch it on.'

He switched on the radio and almost immediately the message from the harbourmaster was broadcast. Sebastian gave a loud cry and his eyes filled with tears. Without wasting a moment he swung the boat around and headed for the coast as quickly as he could.

They arrived in the early hours of the morning while it was still dark. In less time than it takes to tell, Sebastian had tied up the boat and climbed the steep streets of the fishing village to his house.

'Oh, Sebastian!' cried his wife, full

of joy. 'You have come home at last!'

'Nicholas? How is he?' asked Sebastian anxiously.

'He is better now. He has been very ill, but last night he took a turn for the better and the doctor says we have nothing to fear now,' she replied.

'Who is it?' called Nicholas from his bedroom. 'Is it Daddy?'

Then Sebastian ran up the stairs and in a moment Nicholas was in his father's arms.

'I am better now, Daddy,' he said.

'I began to wonder whether you got my message,' said Sebastian's wife. 'You were so long in coming.'

'I never would have heard it had it not been for a swallow,' said Sebastian gravely, and he went to the window and looked out. Surely it must have been a dream; miracles like that of the swallow coming to him did not really happen. But the swallow was real enough. In the dawn light Sebastian saw her busy building her nest under his roof. She looked up and saw Sebastian. He waved to her, smiling.

'Who are you waving to?' asked Nicholas.

'A swallow,' answered Sebastian. 'I waved to our swallow.'

Then he sat on the end of the bed and told his wife and son the whole amazing story.

The Lighthouse in the Moon

Far, far away, on a small island set
in the middle of a great ocean, there
was a lighthouse. The lighthouse keeper
was an old man named Jerome. Every
evening when it began to grow dark,
he would light the lamp, whose yellow
beam shone far out to sea to warn
sailors of the hidden rocks below the
water near the island.

Jerome lived in the lighthouse for many years and, when he was old, angels came and bore away his soul.

When the angels brought Jerome to Heaven, Jesus praised him for his hardworking and honest life and asked what he would like as a reward.

Then Jerome gave a low bow and said, 'Oh, Lord, I would like to live in a lighthouse high up in the sky.'

Jesus looked puzzled.

'But Jerome, in my kingdom there is no ocean, no islands and no sailors,' he said.

'Up here in the sky there is the moon,' Jerome replied. 'Please send me to live there. Each evening I will light the moon and flood all the world with a pale light.'

Jesus smiled kindly at the old man. 'Very well,' he said.

Then he ordered his angels to take Jerome to the moon, and the old man has lived there ever since, reigning in his lighthouse with his lamp of gold.

If you were to look at the moon through a pair of really big glasses, you might see Jerome smiling happily.

Flatbill

All along the river the little ducks were training for the swimming race to be held next day when they would swim before King Swan. But one of them, named Flatbill, did not like the water. He spent his time chasing the insects among the tall grasses on the river-bank.

'Why don't you practise for the race?'

asked the other ducklings as they swam alongside him, panting and breathless.

'Why should I practise? I know that I shall win,' Flatbill replied boastfully.

The day of the race dawned bright and clear. On the river bank King Swan acknowledged the cheers of his subjects. The little ducklings were all lined up ready to dive, and at the end of the row stood Flatbill.

'Look at me! I shall win the race!' he cried.

King Swan fired the starting pistol. All the ducklings dived into the water with a great splash. Flatbill streaked ahead like a rocket. What a sight! Everyone clapped their hands and cheered,

'Go on, Flatbill!'

'Well done, Flatbill!'

29

Flatbill crossed the finishing line well ahead of the others. But as he waded ashore the spectators caught sight of a little motor fixed under his tail! That was how he had won the race! No wonder Flatbill had never practised. He had not had to swim at all. He had gone at full-speed through the water powered by a motor!

King Swan was very, very cross indeed.

'You have cheated, Flatbill,' he said severely. 'And if we had not chanced to catch sight of the motor tucked under your tail, you would have been given first prize for winning the race. It really was most dishonest of you and I am more ashamed than I can say, for you have brought disgrace on all of us with your conduct. As your punishment, I am going to make you spend the rest of the week diving in the river-bed so that you can pull up all the moss and weeds that choke the water here. Perhaps that will teach you to be an honest duck in future!'

The Little Stray Cat

One cold moonlight night a little stray cat wandered through the town, miaowing pitifully with hunger and cold. Suddenly a window opened and a man appeared in his pyjamas with a nightcap on his head.

'Stop that awful noise!' he cried. 'I want to sleep.'

And he threw a bedroom slipper at

the cat. She miaowed all the louder.

Other windows opened and the people, who were cross at being woken up, started to throw things at the cat— books, apples, a lampshade. The little cat was most surprised!

And then, goodness knows why, someone threw down a string of sausages! The cat seized them and ran off, and the street was quiet once more.

But the following night the cat was back again, miaowing as loudly as she could and hoping for more sausages. Each night she sat in the street, keeping everyone awake until they threw down something for her to eat. She had just learnt how to get a free meal!

The Proud Little Ant

One evening the animals of the forest met by the light of the moon and they all began to praise the ant. They made some very beautiful speeches too.

The lion spoke first.

'I admire the ant,' he said, 'because she is so hard-working and because she finds her food without having to kill other creatures.'

The gazelle was the next one to speak.

'Which of us can equal her strength and endurance when travelling?' she asked. 'She can journey thousands of miles carrying a load as big as herself on her back, and when she reaches the anthill she is ready to make the whole journey over again.'

Then it was the snail's turn.

'When danger threatens,' he said, 'she does not curl up in her shell like I do and neither does she follow the example of our friend the ostrich, who buries his head in the sand. The ant, my friends, gathers her armies and organises them in the defence of her anthill, and the ants are some of the bravest fighters in the world.'

Now all this time the ant had been

sitting unnoticed on the elephant's back, and when she heard all the nice things which the other animals had to say about her, she felt very proud indeed.

'My friends,' she said, 'I must thank you for your kind words. It is perfectly true, of course; I am a most remarkable creature—strong, brave, hardworking and very, very wise. In fact, I think that I should become your Queen.' So saying, she took a step forward.

Unfortunately she had not noticed that she was right at the edge of the elephant's back, and she fell to the ground in a most undignified way.

'Pride comes before a fall!' laughed the other animals.

The Story of a Red Balloon

At a fair one day a red balloon escaped from a child's hand and flew up into the wide blue sky.

He was happy to be free and he cried, 'Don't I fly well? Look how high I am!'

He bumped into a passing sparrow and said to him, 'Let's have a race. Let's see who can reach that great white cotton-wool cloud up there first!'

'Don't be silly,' replied the sparrow. 'We could never fly as high as that. That is the land of the angels.'

But the balloon was very obstinate.

'I *will* get there!' he said crossly.

Along came a puff of wind which blew him still higher into the sky.

Presently he met an eagle who asked, 'Where are you going, red balloon?'

'Up there—high into the sky. I am going to sleep on that white cloud when I reach it,' answered the balloon.

'I don't think you will,' replied the eagle, shaking his head. 'Only the angels sleep on the clouds.'

'So much the worse for them!' replied the naughty balloon. 'They are going to have a guest tonight!' And on he flew.

He was so puffed up with pride, however, that he suddenly burst with a terrific *bang!* Instead of being a big red balloon he was now only a limp piece of rag, and he floated down to earth as quickly as he had flown upwards.

And as he fell he heard the sound of mocking laughter rising from the fairground below.

The Bear and the Queen Bee

The bear is the most short-sighted of all the animals in the forest; he walks along slowly, his arms outstretched, peering at the ground. If there were a doctor in the forest he would order the bear to wear glasses.

The bear was not always short-sighted, however. Queen Bee injured his sight in order to punish him for his

greediness. I heard the story from an old hunter from the Black Forest who told it as he sat in the inn drinking his beer.

One day in high summer when the bees' hives were full of honey and sugar, the bear put on his hat and his gloves and left his lair. He walked through the woods until he arrived at the hive of Queen Bee. He found her armed with a wooden spoon and a huge saucepan into which she was busily stirring jonquil petals and the juices of roses and violets.

'Good morning, madam,' said the bear politely. 'What are you making?'

Queen Bee stopped stirring for a moment and replied, 'This is honey, Mr Bear, a most delicious honey; it has a very special, sweet, bee-like flavour.'

She wiped her hot forehead with her dainty wing and said with a sigh, 'This is a very busy time of year for us bees. What with taking the pollen from the flowers, making our combs, kneading the beeswax and mixing the juices in the big saucepans, we hardly have time to turn round.'

The bear licked his lips greedily at the sight of all that honey.

'I should be very honoured if you would allow me to help you,' he said with a little bow. 'I do not like to see Your Majesty working so hard at what would be an easy job for a strong fellow like me. I will stir your honey while you fly into the garden for a breath of fresh air.'

'Oh, how kind you are!' exclaimed Queen Bee gratefully.

'Don't worry about your honey. I know exactly what to do,' said the bear.

The bee thanked him again, spread her wings, and flew off into the garden.

Left alone with the huge saucepan of honey, the bear burst out laughing.

'Ho! ho! How easy it is to outwit a bee!' he chortled.

Then that wicked bear plunged his black snout into the saucepan and drank up all the honey in less time than it takes to tell. Smacking his lips, and still chortling to himself, he ambled out into the forest, stretched himself out on the ground in the shade of a big oak tree and began to snore.

When Queen Bee returned to the hive, she found her saucepan empty and her combs broken. She began to sob bitterly, saying, 'Oh, that wicked bear! How could he trick me like that! This winter my bees will die of hunger and then I will be chased out of the hive in disgrace. Oh, how unhappy I am!'

Then she wiped her eyes on her wing and made up her mind to find the wicked bear and to punish him.

She flew over the forest, looking here and looking there. At last she found the bear, still lying fast asleep in the shade of the oak tree.

'Aha!' buzzed the angry bee. 'There he is! Now to punish him in a way he will never forget!'

Under her wing she carried two tiny

drops of soft beeswax. She flew on to the bear's big black snout and, tiptoeing very gently so as not to wake him, she climbed up to his eyes. Under each eyelid she slipped a drop of wax, which immediately began to harden.

'Goodbye, honey thief,' she cried as she flew away. 'You have been well punished!'

Then the bear woke up and felt the hard wax in his eyes. He rubbed his eyes with his paws, but the beeswax had set fast. He scrambled to his feet, but he could not see where he was going and he hit his head hard against the trunk of the tree.

And the bear has been short-sighted ever since.

The Wicked Wolf

When winter came the towns and the countryside were covered in snow and there was little for the animals to eat. The old wolf became very hungry and he decided to leave the forest and go down to the farm to find food. In the farmyard he saw a building with lighted windows. He peeped inside, and saw twenty little pigs sitting at

their desks while their master, a goat with a long beard, taught them their sums.

The wolf pulled his hat down over his eyes and perched a pair of glasses on his nose. Then he rapped at the door.

'I am the school inspector!' he called. 'Open the door and let me in!'

The pigs grunted excitedly. Perhaps the inspector would give them a day's holiday!

'That is not the inspector's voice!' the goat said to himself.

He bolted and barred the door and peeped out of the window.

He saw a figure in a coat and hat, but under the coat was a long, furry tail—a wolf's tail!

'Wait a moment, sir!' he called. Then he hid behind the classroom door and gently drew back the bolts.

'Come in, Inspector, come in!' he cried, but his legs were set firmly apart and his horns were down.

And when the wolf hurried through the door, licking his lips at the sight of all the fat little pigs, the goat charged at him with his sharp horns! Wham! Bang! The wolf turned three quick somersaults and landed in a heap in the snow.

'Go back to your forest, you wicked wolf!' cried the goat, as he shut and bolted the classroom door once more. The wolf carefully picked himself up and dusted down his jacket. He was very stiff, and battered and bruised all over by the goat's wicked, needle sharp horns.

'I shall certainly not come and try my luck here again,' he muttered to himself as he hurried away to the safety of the forest. 'That schoolmaster goat is much too cunning and fierce!'

Jackie and the Thieving Magpie

When summer came to the mountains, the Belleview Inn in the pretty village of Montfleuri was filled with holiday-makers. Then Jackie, the young shep-herd, came down from his hut high up in the mountains, and was engaged as a servant at the inn. All the guests liked him for he was always smiling and helpful. Every morning he ran down to the shop to buy Colonel Whiskers' paper; he picked bunches of blue gentians for Mrs Honeybun; and he told the children stories of the great mountain that towered above.

Life was happy at the inn until one day a terrible thing happened—the gold watch which the Colonel kept in a special pocket in his waistcoat disappeared.

And that evening, when she came down to dinner, Mrs Honeybun said tearfully that her diamond ring had been stolen from its case.

Then there was panic. Everyone was afraid that their possessions would be the next to be stolen by the mysterious thief. The guests started packing their cases and phoning for taxis to take them away. The landlord was in despair; he would be ruined if all his guests left and spread the tale of the thefts, for then no one else would come to stay. He sent for the village policeman, but the policeman could not help.

Then the landlord called Jackie and said, 'Jackie, you and I must catch this thief or I shall be ruined. The guests are leaving one after the other and they will never set foot in Montfleuri again. Now listen: tonight I will hide in the kitchen and you must hide in the garden. If the thief returns one of us will be sure to see him, and between us we should be able to catch him.'

So that night Jackie went into the garden and crouched down among the

cabbages. All night he watched, but there was no sign of the thief. At last, just as the sun was rising, he saw a movement on one of the balconies. A great black and white magpie, with something shining held in its beak, flew from the balcony to the top of a tall pine tree nearby.

'Aha!' cried Jackie triumphantly. 'So you are the mysterious thief, you wicked bird. The stolen jewellery must be in your nest. I shall soon have it safely.'

Jackie began to climb the pine tree until, at the top he found the magpie's nest. There, among pieces of coloured glass and shiny metal which the magpie had collected, he found the Colonel's watch, Mrs Honeybun's diamond ring and the brooch that the magpie had just stolen that morning. Jackie put the precious things in his pocket, tucked the surprised magpie under one arm, and climbed down the tree again.

When Jackie reached the inn, the landlord thanked him with tears in his eyes and gave him a purseful of money as a reward. The guests praised him and called him a hero. As for the wicked magpie, Jackie could not bear to kill it so it was allowed to go free, and soared away into the clear blue sky.

The King's Banquet

Long ago there lived a king who was renowned for his kind heart and his good sense. When his son and heir was born, the king wanted all his people to share in his joy and he planned an enormous banquet to which his subjects would be invited.

He summoned all the chefs in the kingdom to the palace and told them to cook their most magnificent dishes for the banquet.

'I will give a prize to the man who prepares the most perfect dish,' said the king. 'The prize will be one of my biggest saucepans filled to the brim with pieces of gold.'

The chefs opened their eyes very wide, and immediately set to work, mixing, beating, whisking and basting. Each one was determined that his dish would be the best to be brought before the king. They seasoned and they flavoured, they garnished and they decorated; surely such a collection of wonderful foods was never seen before or since!

After a while, the cooks had time to look around and see what their

companions were doing. They admired each other's work, but secretly each chef thought that his own dish was the best. Then they looked at what the youngest cook had made. It was a plain brown loaf, deliciously crusty and sweet-smelling.

The other cooks roared with laughter.

'Fancy baking an ordinary loaf for the king!' they said. 'Well, you won't win the prize, that's certain.'

At that moment the king entered the kitchen accompanied by his lords and ladies. He walked between the loaded tables looking, tasting and smelling.

'This roast duck is excellent,' he said, 'and I like the jugged hare. What a marvellous cake! And that pudding is a truly amazing sight.'